CTW
SESAME STREET
The Whole Wide World
A Question and Answer Book

By Rae Paige
Illustrated by Tom Cooke
and Jean Zallinger

Includes material from:
The Sesame Street Question and Answer Book About Animals
and *Big Bird's Book About the Earth and Sky*

A SESAME STREET/GOLDEN PRESS BOOK

Published by Western Publishing Company, Inc.
in conjunction with Children's Television Workshop.

Consultants

George Fichter
Naturalist and Biologist

David Parsons
Chief Exhibit Preparator
Peabody Museum, Yale University

Dr. William A. Gutsch, Jr.
Chairman, American Museum—Hayden Planetarium

Table of Contents

What Is the Earth?

"Hi, there! This is the Earth! Isn't it beautiful?"

What is the Earth?
The Earth is the planet we live on. It is also called the world.

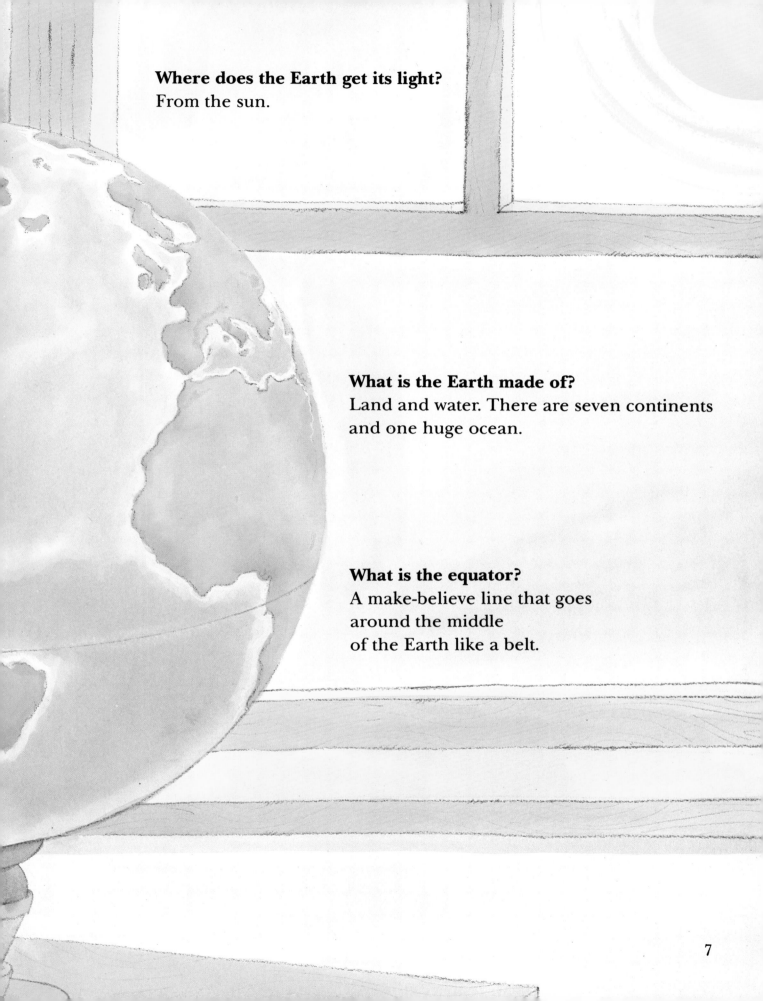

Where does the Earth get its light?
From the sun.

What is the Earth made of?
Land and water. There are seven continents
and one huge ocean.

What is the equator?
A make-believe line that goes
around the middle
of the Earth like a belt.

What Animals Lay Eggs?

Many animals—
not just birds—lay eggs.
Turtles, frogs,
some snakes, fishes, bees,
ants, snails, platypuses,
alligators, and crocodiles are
just a few of the
many animals that lay eggs.
Even dinosaurs
came from eggs.

8

Are all eggs white?
No. Many are naturally blue, pink, green,
brown, and speckled brown, gray, and black.
And then there are Easter eggs!

Emperor penguins have a special
way of taking care of their eggs.
After the mother lays the egg, the
father keeps it warm in a
fold of skin just above his feet.

What is the smallest bird egg?
The smallest bird egg in the world
is the hummingbird egg.
It's about the size of a raisin.

What is the biggest egg?
The biggest egg
in the world
is the ostrich egg.
It's as big as a
large grapefruit.

"They don't, Ernie. Chickens lay their
eggs in nests. Farmers gather the
eggs and put them in cartons."

"Hey, Bert. How do chickens lay
their eggs inside those little
cardboard egg cartons?"

What Are Baby Animals Called?

"Hmm. It says in this book a baby owl is called an owlet. What do we call a baby grouch, Oscar?"

"A grouchlet, of course."

piglet

chicks

calves

cubs

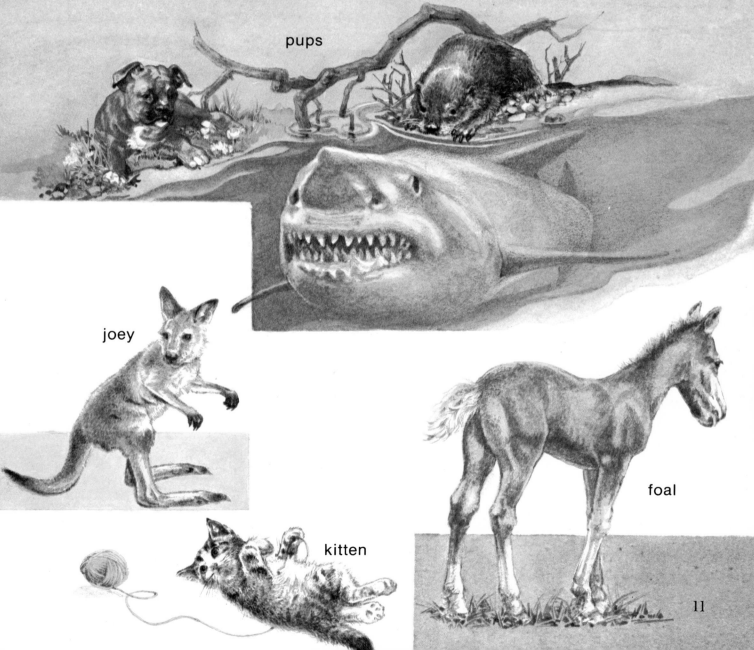

pups

joey

foal

kitten

11

What Do Baby Animals Look Like?

Some babies look like
their parents, only smaller.

tigers

dolphins

lions

12

dogs

zebras

swans

Some babies don't look like
their parents at all.

butterfly

caterpillar

frog

tadpole

How Do Parents Carry Their Babies?

Parents carry their babies around in many different ways.

A baby kangaroo lives in its mother's pouch for about six months.

A monkey parent can swing through the trees with a baby monkey hanging onto its neck.

A beaver parent sometimes carries its baby cradled in its arms.

Young opossums
hold on to their mother's
fur as she walks.

Human babies sometimes ride
on their parent's back, too.

A father sea horse carries
sea horse eggs in a pouch
until the eggs hatch.

A mother cat
sometimes carries her kitten
by the scruff of its neck.

A baby
hippopotamus
rides on its
mother's back
in the water.

True or False?

Raccoons roast their corn before they eat it.
True or false?

FALSE. But they do sometimes dunk their
food in water before they eat it.

Penguins like to go sledding.
True or false?

TRUE. They slide down
snowy hills
on their stomachs.

Elephants wear hats. True or false?

TRUE. Elephants sometimes make hats of wet grass and mud to keep the hot sun off their heads.

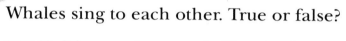

Whales sing to each other. True or false?

TRUE. They make sounds like singing that seem to "tell" things to other whales.

Bulls charge at a red cape because they hate red. True or false?

FALSE. Bulls are color-blind and can't tell red from any other color. Bulls charge at a cape waving in front of them because of its movement, not its color.

Gorillas like to play checkers and chess. True or false?

FALSE. But baby gorillas play games very much like follow the leader and king of the mountain.

Who Lives in the Sea?

Many animals live underwater.

sea horse

lobster

clam

sponge

starfish

squid

dolphin

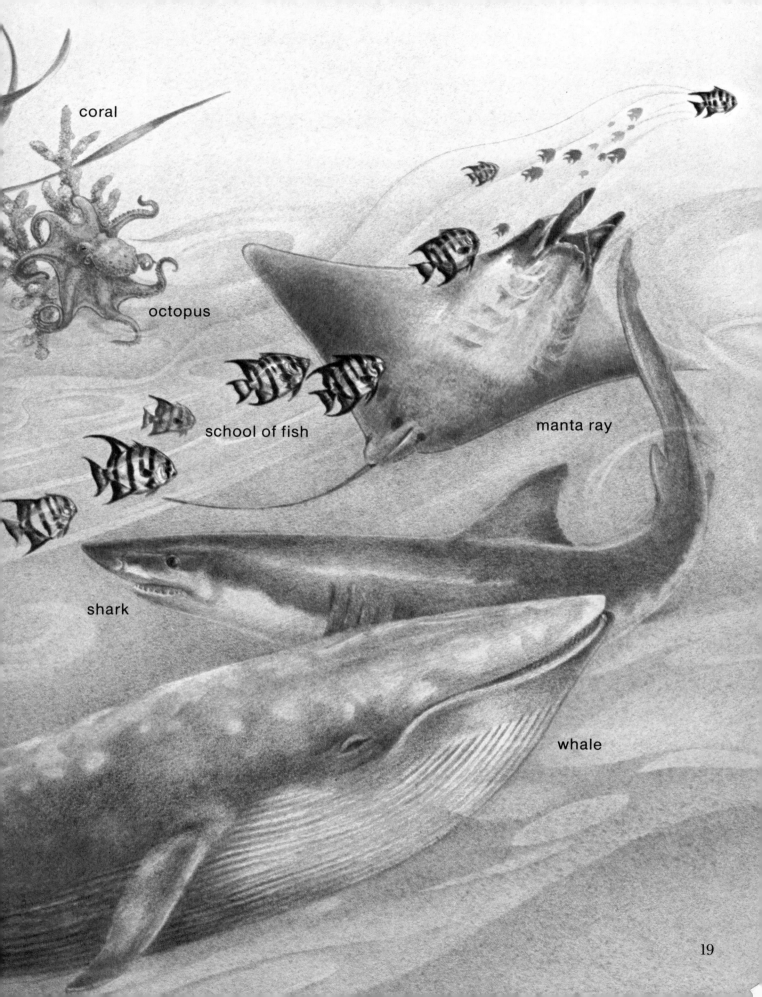

coral

octopus

school of fish

manta ray

shark

whale

19

Who's Winning?

These animals are all crawling, running, hopping, flying, galloping, or swimming as fast as they can. Who do you think will win the race?

hawk
35 mph (miles per hour)

elephant
25 mph

giraffe
32 mph

reindeer
32 mph

racehorse
47 mph

person
27 mph

greyhound
39 mph

cat
30 mph

snail
1½ miles per week

rabbit
35 mph

penguin
30 mph

blue whale
25 mph

dolphin
37 mph

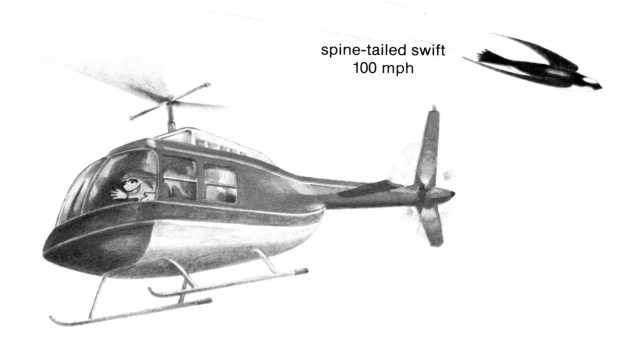

spine-tailed swift
100 mph

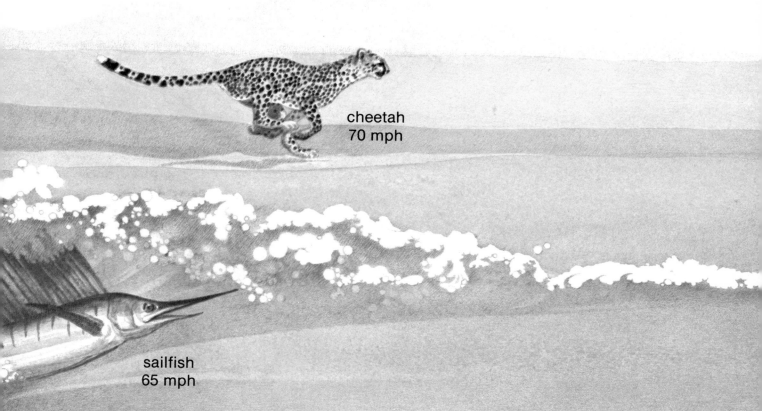

cheetah
70 mph

sailfish
65 mph

Bats and...

"Greetings! I am the Count. Let me introduce you to my wonderful, beautiful bats!"

Bats are the only animals besides birds and insects that can fly. Most bats fly at night and sleep all day, hanging by their feet in caves or other dark places.

How do bats fly at night without bumping into things?
Bats have a special kind of hearing which helps them sense where things are, even when they can't see them.

Are bats really blind?
No. Many people think that bats are blind, but bats really have good eyesight.

...Cats

"Here, kitty, kitty, kitty! I like pussycats because they have soft fur just like mine. Yah!"

How can you tell if a cat is scared?
When a cat is frightened, it hisses, arches its back, and puffs up its fur.

Why do cats lick themselves?
To get clean. Cats lick themselves all over with their scratchy tongues to clean their fur. They wash their faces and their ears by licking their paws and using them as washcloths.

How do cats climb trees?
By digging their claws into the bark of the tree. Cats also use their claws as weapons.

Is it true that cats have nine lives?
No. People just say that because cats have a knack for getting out of danger.

Can cats see in the dark?
Cats are able to see in very dim light but not in complete darkness.

23

Big Bird's Bird Questions

"A bird is an animal with feathers, two wings, two legs, a beak, and no teeth. Isn't he adorable?"

HOME TWEET HOME

Can all birds fly?
No. Penguins and ostriches and some other birds can't fly because their wings are too small.

Are bald eagles really bald?
No. They just look that way
from a distance because the
feathers on their heads
are a very light color.

Why do woodpeckers peck on trees?
They eat the little insects that live in the bark.

**Why don't woodpeckers get headaches
when they peck on trees?**
Because they have very hard bills and special
padding in their heads.

"Hey, Ern, why do
hummingbirds hum?"

"Because they don't
know the words, Bert?"

"No, Ernie.
When hummingbirds fly,
their wings beat
very fast and make
a humming sound."

Oscar's Yucchy Questions

What does a camel do when it's grouchy?
It spits.

Why do pigs roll around in the mud?
To keep cool.

Do goats eat tin cans?
No, but they chew on them because they like the taste of the glue that holds the labels on the cans.

What does a skunk do when it's afraid?
It sprays a stinky mist toward its enemy.

How can you get rid of skunk smell?
Scrub anything skunky with tomato juice, soap, and water.

"Hey! Who wants to get rid of it?"

How Many?

"Greetings! Can you tell me how many?"

How many feet does a snail have?
One. One foot.

How many arms does an octopus have?
Eight. Eight arms.

How many arms does a starfish have?
Five. Five arms.

How many legs does a spider have?
Eight. Eight legs.

How many legs does a ladybug have?
Six. Six legs.

How many legs does a centipede have?
Most centipedes have 35 pairs of legs, or 70 legs in all. Seventy legs.

How many heads does a two-headed monster have?
Two. Two heads!

Small World

"Here are some of the smallest animals in the world."

dwarf pygmy goby fish
It's tinier than a thimble.

bee hummingbird
It's as small as a walnut.

bumblebee bat
Its body is as small
as a peach pit.

itchmite
The itchmite is so small
that you can't see it.

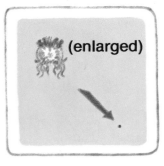

(enlarged)

pygmy shrew
It would fit in the palm
of a small child's hand.

Big News

"Here's some big news."

What is the biggest animal of all?

The blue whale. It weighs as much as a locomotive. It's the biggest animal that has ever lived, even bigger than a dinosaur!

What's the biggest cat?

The biggest member of the cat family is the tiger. A tiger grows to be more than ten feet long from the tip of its nose to the tip of its tail. It weighs as much as four grown-ups.

What is the biggest land animal?

The African elephant. It weighs as much as two cars.

What is the biggest bird?

The ostrich is the biggest bird in the world. It's as tall as a very big bear.

29

What's for Dinner?

"What do Cookie Monsters really eat? Cuppy cakes. (And fruits and vegetables, and cheese and meat.)"

Some snakes can unhinge their jaw to swallow an egg larger than the width of their body.

Pelicans catch fish for dinner.

An anteater sticks out his long tongue to lick up ants and other insects.

Cows and horses eat grass.

Giraffes eat leaves from the tip-tops of acacia trees.

Flamingos eat with their heads upside down. They filter mud with their beaks to find tiny bugs.

How Do Animals Sleep?

"Time for sweet dreams."

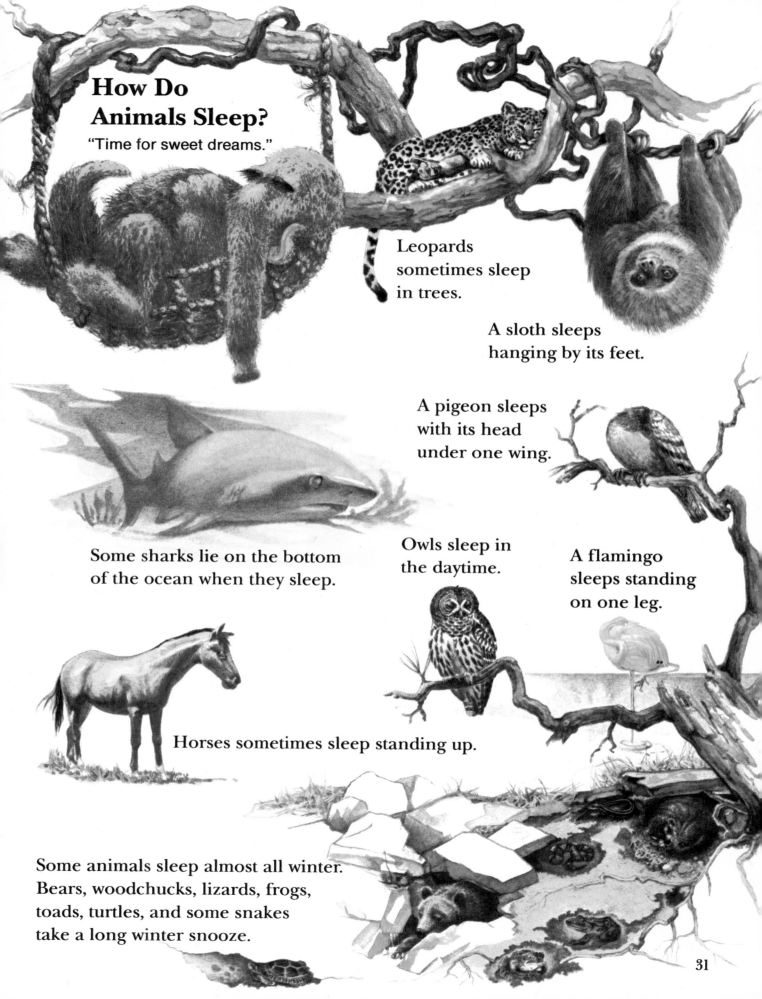

Leopards sometimes sleep in trees.

A sloth sleeps hanging by its feet.

A pigeon sleeps with its head under one wing.

Some sharks lie on the bottom of the ocean when they sleep.

Owls sleep in the daytime.

A flamingo sleeps standing on one leg.

Horses sometimes sleep standing up.

Some animals sleep almost all winter. Bears, woodchucks, lizards, frogs, toads, turtles, and some snakes take a long winter snooze.

Hard Facts About Bones

Not all animals have bones.
Jellyfish don't have bones. Neither do
worms, spiders or insects.

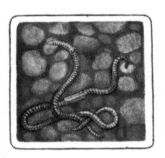  

Do birds have bones?
Yes. One reason birds can fly is that
their bones are light and filled with air.

BIRD

ANATOSAURUS
(DUCK-BILLED DINOSAUR)
NO. AMERICA

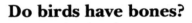
DINOSAUR THIGH BONE

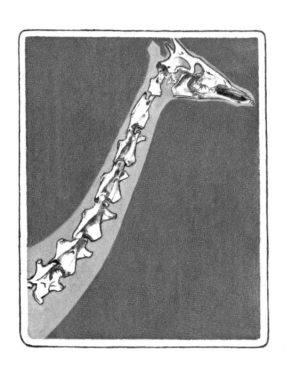

A giraffe has seven bones in its neck.
A sparrow has fourteen bones in its neck.

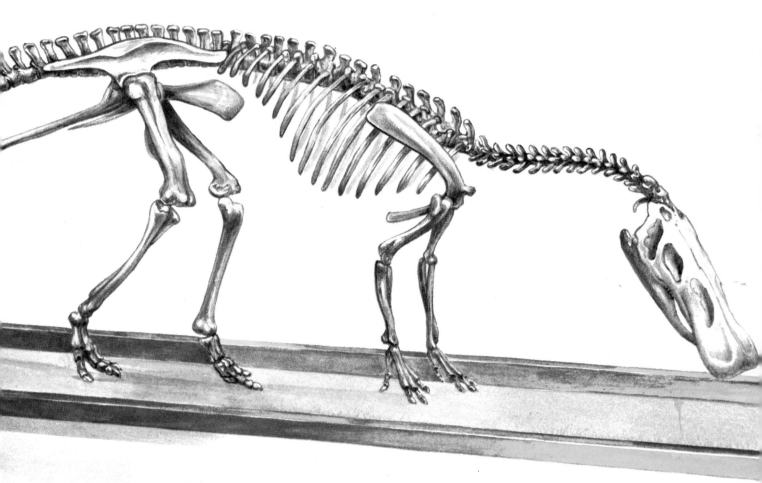

Dinosaurs had huge bones. Dinosaurs lived
millions of years ago, and all that is left of them
is their bones.

Have You Heard?

Kangaroos are excellent swimmers.

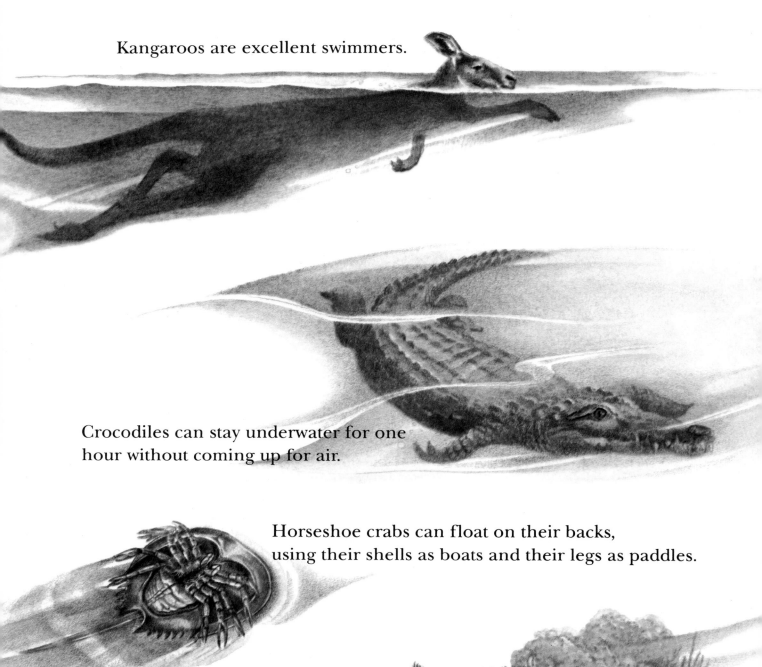

Crocodiles can stay underwater for one
hour without coming up for air.

Horseshoe crabs can float on their backs,
using their shells as boats and their legs as paddles.

Batfish crawl along the bottom of
the ocean instead of swimming.

Gorillas make nests in trees just like birds. But gorillas don't lay eggs in their nests; they sleep in them.

Seashells are the hard outer covering of some sea animals. When the animals die, their shells may be washed onto the shore.

Lantern fish live where it's dark, and they can make their own light.

"That is so they can see in the middle of the night when they get up for a glass of water."

35

How Do Animals Use Their Tails?

Beavers use their tails to pack down mud on their dams.

Beavers slap their tails on the water to warn other beavers of danger.

Kangaroos use their tails to push themselves off the ground when they jump.

36

Cows and horses use their
tails as flyswatters.

Opossums use their tails
to hang from branches.

Some monkeys swing from
tree branches by their tails.

Fish swim by pushing
themselves through the water
with their tails.

Rivers, Lakes, and Ponds

Rivers, lakes, and ponds are the homes of
many kinds of fish, frogs, insects, snakes, ducks,
turtles, and geese. Also, many different plants live
in water.

What is a river?
A large stream of fresh,
not salty, water.

What is a lake?
A large body of water that collects in a low place in the ground.

What is a pond?
A small lake.

Mountains

"Hello, everybody!
It is I, Grover, on top
of a mountain."

What are mountains?
Very high hills. Some mountains are steep and rocky. Other mountains are round and covered with trees. Mountain goats, eagles, snow leopards, elks, and other animals live on the mountains.

What is the highest mountain in the world?
Mount Everest, in Nepal.

What is a volcano?
A mountain that gushes rock so hot that it runs like a river.

Caves

What are caves?
Hollow spaces underneath the ground. Caves are carved by wind, waves, lava, ice, or dripping water. Bats live in caves.

"Look at this, Ernie. This is a stalactite. It grows down from the top of the cave."

"That's nothing, Bert. Look at this! This is a stalagmite. It grows up from the ground."

Carlsbad Caverns

Deserts

What is a desert?

A very, very dry place. Rattlesnakes, lizards, rabbits, coyotes, and other animals live in the desert.

What is a cactus?

A desert plant that grows in sand and can live with very little water. Cactus plants have thorns instead of leaves. A cactus stores all its water in its body. Some cacti can go a year without water.

"I love the desert. There are sooo many grains of sand to count.... One billion one tiny grains of sand, one billion two tiny grains of sand...."

What is sand?

Itsy-bitsy, teeny-tiny pieces of rock.

Swamps

What is a swamp?
Soggy, wet land. Flamingos, water moccasins, alligators, snapping turtles, and other animals live in swamps.

"I love swamps. Everything's so wet and slimy and yucchy. Speaking of Slimey, he loves it too!"

What is the largest swamp in the world?
The Everglades in Florida.

Jungles

What is a jungle?

A warm, wet forest with many large trees. Elephants, monkeys, parrots, pythons, and other animals live in the jungle. There are more kinds of trees in the jungle than anywhere else on the Earth.

"There are more insects in the jungle than anywhere else, too."

Icebergs

What is an iceberg?

A huge chunk of ice floating in the ocean. Most of an iceberg is underwater. Only the tip of it shows.

"Seals like to rest on icebergs. Yah!"

How Do People Live Around the World?

Most people live in places where it's cold in the winter and warm in the summer. They wear lots of clothes in the winter and few clothes in the summer.

People who live in cold parts of the world, like Alaska, have to dress to keep warm.

People who live in warm parts of the world, like Hawaii, dress to stay cool.

People who live in the Sahara Desert wear long robes and head coverings to protect themselves from the wind and heat.

Trees

"Greetings! If you count the rings in a tree trunk, you can tell the age of the tree. There's one ring for each year. Let's count. One ring, two rings, three rings, four... This tree is four rings, I mean four years, old!"

leaves

branches

Leaves come in all different shapes and sizes, just as trees do.

"This is my leaf collection. Can you make one, too? How many different kinds of leaves can you find where you live?"

trunk

roots

palm

maple

gingko

oak

mimosa

Flowers

"My mommy will love these beautiful and adorable flowers."

How does your garden grow?
Soil, sunlight, and rain
make plants and flowers grow.

rose

daisy

There are many, many different kinds of flowers.
They grow almost everywhere. Some flowers
have a sweet smell.

carnation

lily

pansy

Does Pizza Grow on Trees?

"Oh, I am so excited!
I love yummy fresh vegetables!"

Where does cheese come from?
Cheese is made from milk.

tomato

pepper

onion

Where does flour come from?
Some flour comes from wheat. The wheat is
ground up in a mill that turns it into flour.

Where do tomatoes and peppers come from?
Plants that grow in the ground.

What about onions?
Onions grow underground in the soil.

"Hey, everybody!
With all these delicious things—flour,
tomatoes, peppers, onions, and cheese—
I can make PIZZA!"

Flour

Do Cookies Grow on Trees?

Where does milk come from?
Cows. Mother cows make milk
in their bodies. Farmers milk the cows
and send the milk to a dairy
where it is put into bottles
or cartons.

Where does butter come from?
Milk. Grover's great-grandmother used to make
butter in a wooden churn. Now machines do it.

Where does honey come from?
Bees make it from flower nectar, a sweet juice
in flowers. They store it in honeycomb,
which is made out of beeswax.

Where does chocolate come from?
Beans that grow on a tree called the cacao tree.

Where do eggs come from?
Chickens lay eggs.

Where does vanilla come from?
Vanilla beans, which grow on a climbing orchid plant.

"Hmmm. Milk…butter… honey…chocolate…eggs… vanilla…flour. That's where COOOOKIES come from!"

53

The Ocean

What is the ocean?
The water that covers most of the Earth.

What is a beach?
A sandy place at the edge of the ocean.

Why is the ocean salty?
Rain washes salt from the earth and carries it to the ocean. People shouldn't drink ocean water because the salty water will make them more thirsty.

What makes waves?
Wind blowing across the water makes waves.

Guy Smiley's Wonderful Weather Show

Weather Show

This is Guy Smiley, the world's favorite game show host, welcoming you to the WONDERFUL WEATHER SHOW! Yeah!

The first question is:
What's all around you but can't be seen, tasted, or smelled?
Air! That's right. The air you breathe. Here's a jar of it.

The second question is:

What is a cloud?

And the answer is: billions of tiny drops of water and tiny specks of dust that float in the air.

And now,

What is wind?

Right! You're right! Wind is moving air. The only time you can feel air is when it's windy! A storm called a hurricane brings very strong winds.

What is a tornado?

A funnel-shaped cloud with very strong, swirling winds.

The next question is:
What is rain?
Drops of water which fall from the clouds.

What is a flash of light in the sky during a rainstorm?
It's lightning, caused by electricity in the air.

What is the noise you usually hear after a flash of lightning?
How did you know? YES! It's THUNDER!

And now, FOR THE GRAND PRIZE, the last question is:
What is snow?
Water in clouds that freezes and falls to the earth as snowflakes. You did it! You won! So here's your prize from GUY SMILEY'S WONDERFUL WEATHER SHOW...a year's supply, that is 365 days, of... FREE WEATHER!

"Did you know that no two snowflakes are exactly alike?"

"Right. Hold out your mitten and look closely. See? Each snowflake is different."

Over the Rainbow

"Howdy, pardner! Sometimes when I'm out riding the range, I see beautiful rainbows."

What is a rainbow?
A rainbow forms when light shines through raindrops. A rainbow usually means that a storm is over, but you might see a rainbow when rain is falling and the sun is shining at the same time.

What are all the colors in the rainbow?
Red, orange, yellow, green, blue, and violet. Light is made up of these colors, but you usually can't see all of them.

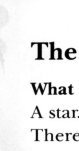

The Sun

What is the sun?
A star. It is the closest star to Earth.
There could be no life on Earth
without the light and heat
from the sun.

What is day?
It is day on the side of the Earth that faces the sun.
If the sky isn't cloudy, the people on this side of
the Earth can see the sunlight.

"Did you know, Tina,
that you should never
look directly at the sun,
even when you're wearing
sunglasses?"

"That's true, Tessie.
It's very bad
for your eyes."

The Moon

What is the moon?

The large white ball we see in the sky. It is made of moon rocks and soil. It has mountains, valleys, plains, and lots of craters. Since the moon has no air, food, or water, there is no life on the moon.

Where does the moon get its light?

We can see the moon because the sun's light shines on it.

What is night?

It is night on the side of the Earth that is facing away from the sun. If the sky isn't cloudy, the people on this side of the Earth can see the stars.

"Is there a man on the moon, Bert?"

"Just you and me, Ernie."

Stars

What is a star?
A huge burning ball of fire. Our sun is a star.

What is the Milky Way?
A huge group of stars that is called a galaxy. Sometimes you can see the Milky Way as a band of light in the night sky.

The Little Dipper looks like a little spoon. The star at the end of the Little Dipper's handle is called the North Star.

The Big Dipper is a group of seven stars that looks like a ladle or a big spoon.

What is a constellation?
A group of stars that forms a pattern or picture.

"And what constellation
is that, Tina?"

"Can't you tell?
That's Cookie Monster."

65

Astro-Bird

"Look at me, everybody!
I'm an astro-bird!"

What are astronauts?
They are space explorers
who blast off to outer
space in spacecraft.

Why do astronauts wear space suits?
Because they have to take their own air with
them. Space suits supply the astronauts with air,
and, like big snowsuits, also keep them warm.

Blast-off

Ten, nine, eight, seven, six,
five, four, three, two,
one...BLAST OFF!

Astronauts do not weigh anything
when they are in space. If they don't
wear their seat belts, they float around
in the spacecraft.

The Solar System

What is the solar system?
The sun and the nine planets that travel around the sun.

Pluto

Uranus

Neptune

Saturn

Mars

Venus

Earth